LIEBESTRÄUME

(NOCTURNE No. 3)

Franz Liszt (1811–1886)
Grove 541/3; Raabe 211/3

Poco allegro, con affetto

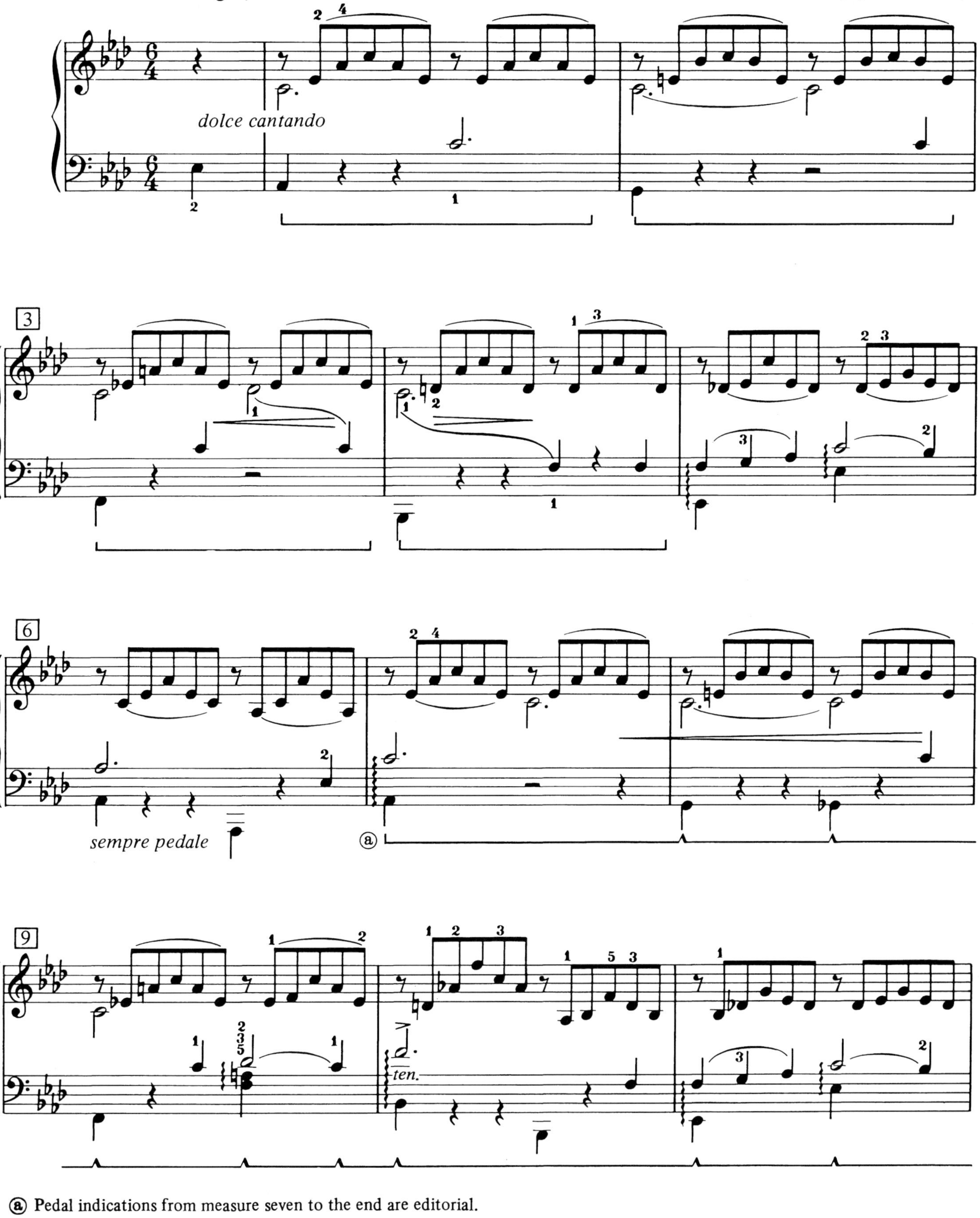

ⓐ Pedal indications from measure seven to the end are editorial.

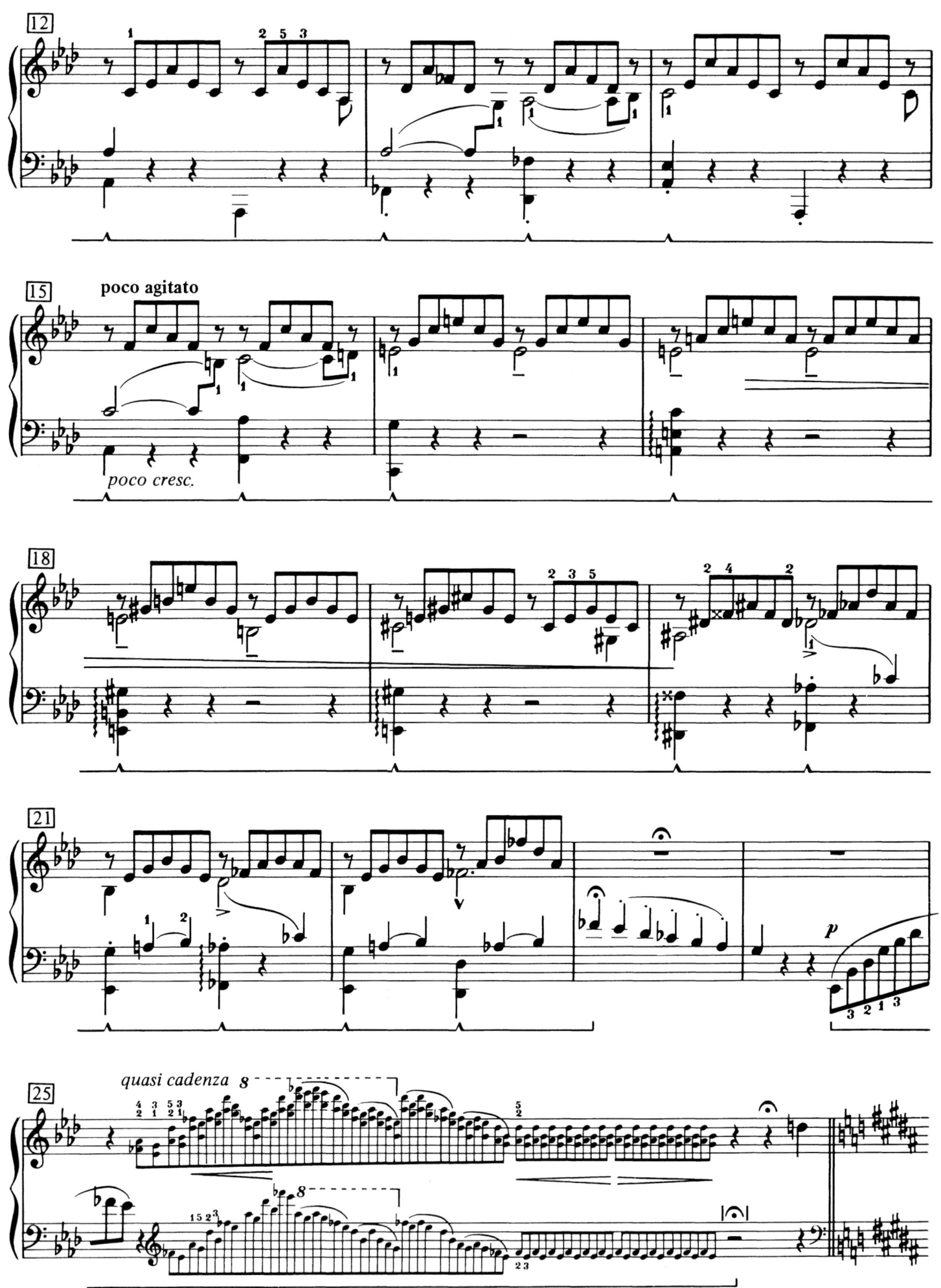

Alfred Masterwork Library
Most Requested

Bach/18 Short Preludes
(Palmer)
Book (601)
CD (rec. K. O'Reilly) (16790)

Bach/Dances of J. S. Bach (Hinson) (600)

Bach/French Suites (Schneider) (700)

Bach/Two-Part Inventions (Palmer) (604)

**Bach/Inventions and Sinfonias
(Two- and Three-Part Inventions)** (Palmer)
Leather (4867)
Paper (Comb-bound) (606C)
CD (rec. Lloyd-Watts) (4056)

Bach/Selections from Anna Magdalena's Notebook
(Palmer)
Book (605)
CD (rec. Lloyd-Watts) (16792)

Bach/Well-Tempered Clavier, Volume 1
(Palmer) (2098C)

Beethoven/16 of His Easiest Piano Selections (383)

**Beethoven/13 of His Most Popular
Piano Selections** (390)

**Beethoven/Selected Intermediate to Early Advanced
Piano Sonata Movements** (Hinson)
Volume 1 (4841)
Volume 2 (4842)

Burgmüller/18 Characteristic Studies, Op. 109
(Hinson) (4829)

Burgmüller/25 Progressive Pieces, Op. 100 (Palmer)
Book (608)
CD (rec. Lloyd-Watts) (16787)

Chopin/14 of His Easiest Piano Selections (397)

**Chopin/19 of His Most Popular
Piano Selections** (389)

Chopin/Etudes, Complete (Palmer) (2500C)

Chopin/An Introduction to His Piano Works (Palmer)
Book (635)
CD (rec. Lloyd-Watts) (4013)

Chopin/Mazurkas (Palmer) (2481)

Chopin/Nocturnes (Palmer) (2482C)

Chopin/Polonaises, Complete (Palmer) (2480C)

Chopin/Preludes (Palmer) (610)

Chopin/Selected Favorites (Palmer) (611)

Chopin/Waltzes (Palmer) (2483)

Clementi/Six Sonatinas, Op. 36 (Palmer)
Book (609)
CD (rec. K. O'Reilly) (16771)

Czerny/30 New Studies in Technique, Op. 849
(Palmer) (591)

**Czerny/Practical Method for Beginners on
the Piano, Op. 599, Complete** (Palmer) (596)

**Czerny/The Art of Finger Dexterity,
Op. 740, Complete** (Palmer) (595C)

Czerny/The School of Velocity, Op. 299 (Palmer)
Book 1 (613)
Complete (612)

Czerny/The Young Pianist, Op. 823, Complete
(Palmer) (590)

Czerny/Selected Piano Studies, Volume 1
(Germer/Palmer) (597)

Debussy/Children's Corner Suite (Hinson) (667)

Debussy/Preludes, Book 1 (Hinson) (2594)

Debussy/Preludes, Book 2 (Hinson) (2598)

Debussy/Selected Favorites (Olson) (2495)

Hanon/The Virtuoso Pianist (Small)
Book 1 (617)
Book 2 (682)
Complete Edition (616C)
GM Disk, Book 1 (arr. Wren) (5715)

Hanon/Junior Hanon (Small) (518)

Köhler/Sonatina Album (Small)
Book (1710C)
Two CDs (rec. K. O'Reilly) (3997)

**Kuhlau/Nine Sonatinas, Opp. 20 and 55
for the Piano** (Palmer) (4889)

Mendelssohn/Songs without Words, Complete
(Hinson) (4860C)

Mozart/14 of His Easiest Pieces (384)

Mozart/21 of His Most Popular Pieces
(Palmer) (391)

**Mozart/Selected Intermediate to Early Advanced
Piano Sonata Movements** (Hinson) (4884)

Mozart/Six "Viennese" Sonatinas (Palmer) (1707)

Rachmaninoff/10 Preludes, Op. 23 (Baylor) (515)

Rachmaninoff/13 Preludes, Op. 32 (Baylor) (655)

Rachmaninoff/Selected Works (Baylor) (2423)

Satie/Gymnopédies and Gnossiennes (Baylor) (2501)

Schmitt/Preparatory Exercises, Op. 16 (Palmer) (1709)

Schubert/Impromptus, Op. 90 (Baylor) (544)

Schumann/Album for the Young, Op. 68 (Palmer)
Book (620)
Two CDs (rec. K. O'Reilly) (16796)

Schumann/Scenes from Childhood, Op. 15 (Palmer)
Book (632)
CD (rec. Lloyd-Watts) (16794)

Streabbog/12 Melodious Pieces, Book 1, Op. 63
(Palmer) (621)

Tchaikovsky/The Nutcracker Suite, Op. 71a (Hinson)
Duet, 1 Piano/4 Hands (4858)
Solo Piano (4856)
CD (rec. Reed/Reed) (16774)

Tchaikovsky/The Seasons, Op. 37b (Hinson) (4826)

Tchaikovsky/Album for the Young, Op. 39 (Novik) (485)

Tcherepnin/Bagatelles, Op. 5 (Olson) (551)

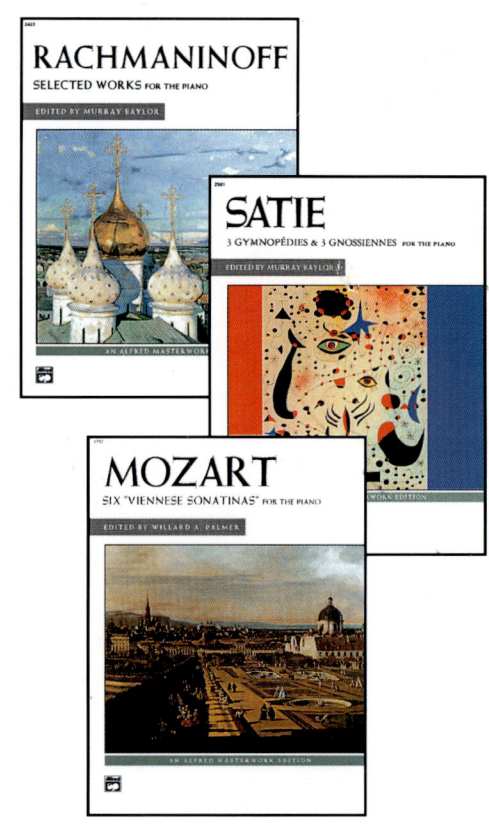

ISBN-10: 0-7390-1874-4
ISBN-13: 978-0-7390-1874-3

alfred.com

896     $4.99 in USA
ISBN 0-7390-1874-4